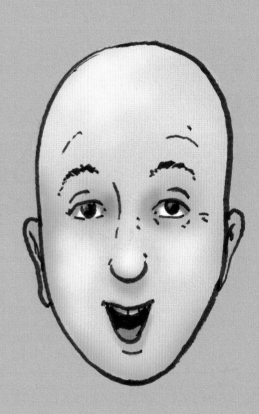

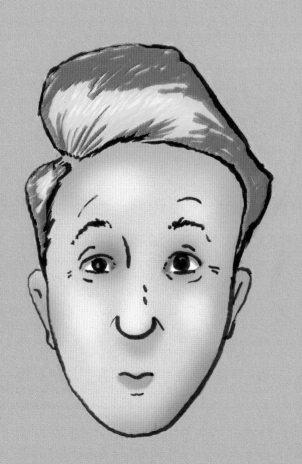

DAD'S BALD HEAD

Paul Many

Illustrations by Kevin O'Malley

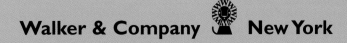

Walker & Company New York

Text copyright © 2007 by Paul Many
Illustrations copyright © 2007 by Kevin O'Malley

First published in the United States of America in 2007 by Walker Publishing Company, Inc.
Distributed to the trade by Holtzbrinck Publishers

For information about permission to reproduce selections from this book, write to Permissions,
Walker & Company, 104 Fifth Avenue, New York, New York 10011

Library of Congress Cataloging-in-Publication Data
Many, Paul.
Dad's bald head / Paul Many ; illustrations by Kevin O'Malley.
p.   cm.
Summary: Pete and his Dad do everything together in the morning except comb their hair, but when
Dad shaves off the last few stragglers it takes Pete some time to adjust to his father's new look.
ISBN-13: 978-0-8027-9579-3 • ISBN-10: 0-8027-9579-X (hardcover)
ISBN-13: 978-0-8027-9580-9 • ISBN-10: 0-8027-9580-3 (reinforced)
[1. Hair—Fiction. 2. Baldness—Fiction. 3. Fathers and sons—Fiction.] I. O'Malley, Kevin. II. Title.
PZZM3212Da 2007   [E]—dc22   2006025088

Typeset in Imperfect Regular
The illustrations for this book were made with brush and ink
on Bond paper and then digitally colored.
Book design by Patrick Collins

Visit Walker & Company's Web site at www.walkeryoungreaders.com

Printed in China

2 4 6 8 10 9 7 5 3 1

All papers used by Walker & Company are natural, recyclable products
made from wood grown in well-managed forests. The manufacturing processes
conform to the environmental regulations of the country of origin.

To the memory of my father, Paul Sr.,
who by his own proud example taught me
everything I know about balding.
—P. M.

For my bald buddy Buzz
—K. O.

Every morning Pete and his dad got up together.

They walked down the hall to the bathroom together.

They washed their faces together.

They brushed their teeth together.

But when it came to combing hair, Pete had to comb his alone.

For Pete's dad had very little hair to comb.

What he did have made Pete think of the way Mr. Samson looked after he'd tumbled around in the dryer.

Sometimes Pete would help his dad. He would use both hands to squash down the scraggly hairs.

"Thanks, kiddo," Dad would say. "With a son like you, who needs a comb?"

But then . . . *sproing*! The wiry hairs always popped right back up again.

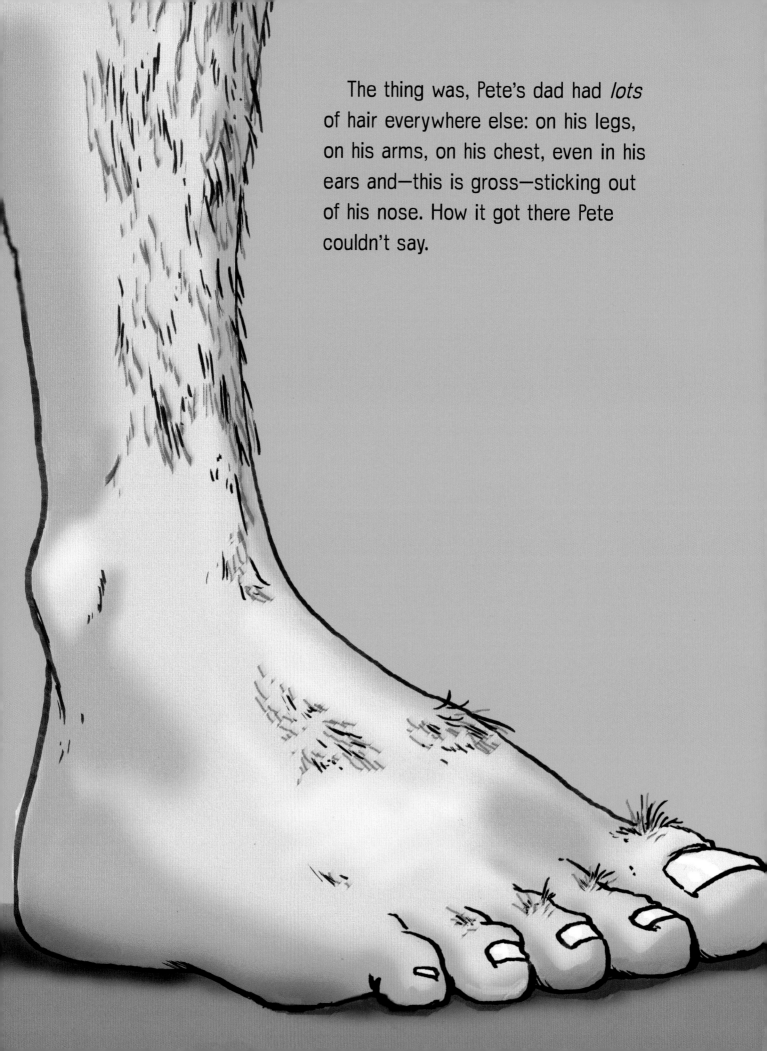

The thing was, Pete's dad had *lots* of hair everywhere else: on his legs, on his arms, on his chest, even in his ears and—this is gross—sticking out of his nose. How it got there Pete couldn't say.

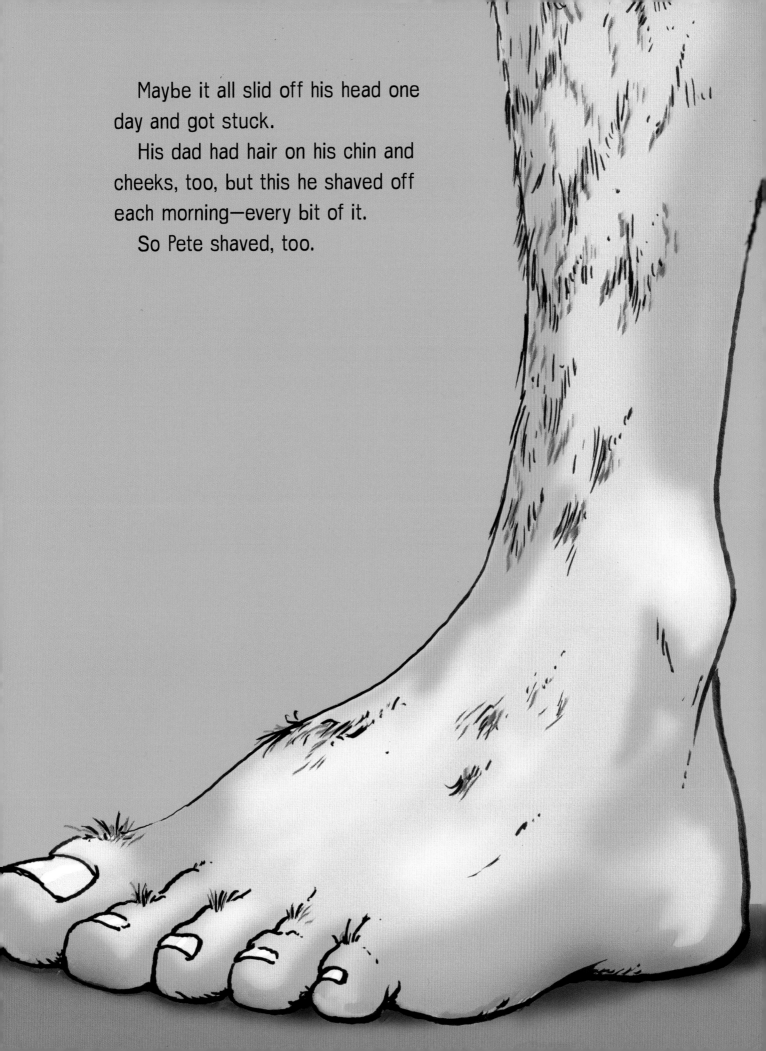

Maybe it all slid off his head one day and got stuck.

His dad had hair on his chin and cheeks, too, but this he shaved off each morning—every bit of it.

So Pete shaved, too.

They slathered up their cheeks and chins with big, gooey Santa Claus beards and squirted thick, fluffy Santa Claus mustaches under their noses.

That part always made Pete sneeze.

"Gesundheit!" Dad would say, and then he'd put a dab of shaving cream right on the tip of Pete's nose.

But one morning Pete's dad did something really weird. He squirted a big blob of shaving cream on the top of his head.

Pete laughed. Dad was always making jokes.

But then Dad did something that surprised Pete so much, he dropped his razor.

When he was through with his chin and cheeks, Dad

just

kept

right

on

shaving.

"Stop, Dad! What are you *doing*?" said Pete. But it was too late.

Dad had shaved off *every single one* of the scrawny hairs on his head.

"Well, what do you think?" he asked Pete.

Pete didn't know what to think. His dad looked so different.

He didn't even look like his dad anymore.

It was kind of scary.

Dad smiled his old smile and wiped the rest of the shaving cream off Pete's face.

"Time to put on the old feedbag, champ," he said.

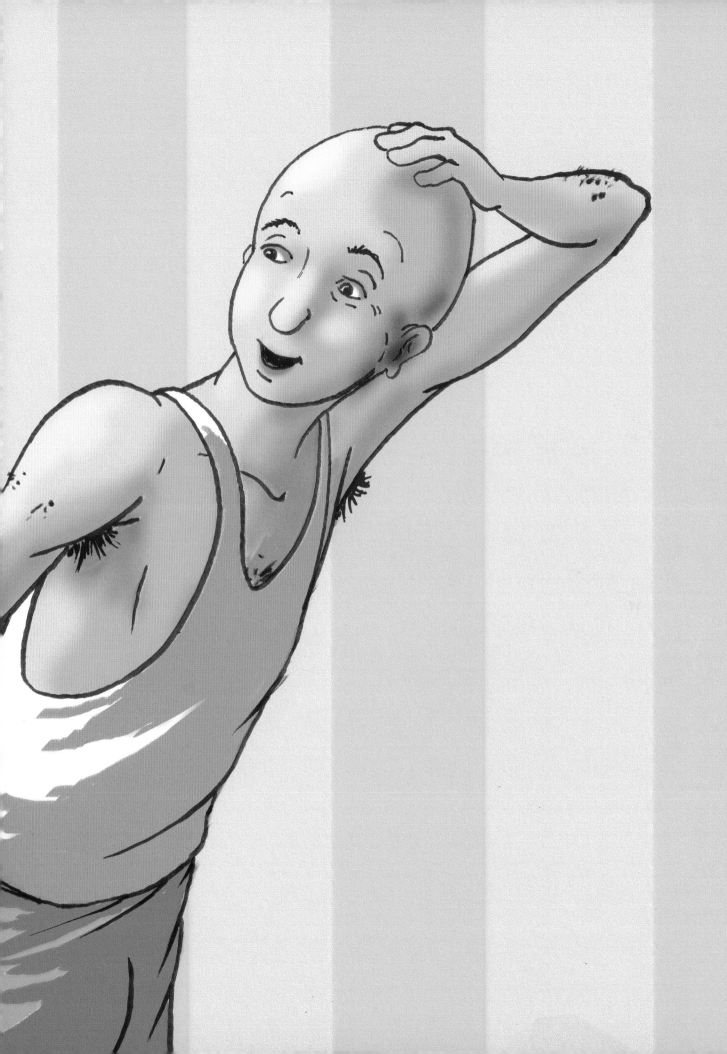

When they came downstairs, Pete's mom said, "Pete,
would you please tell your father it's time for breakfast?"
"He's right here, Mom!" said Pete. "Can't you see him?"

"Who?" she said. "That bald, handsome man over there?"

"It's Dad!" said Pete. "He shaved off all his hair!"

Pete's mother smiled. "Well, so it is, and so he did." She gave Dad a big, smoochy kiss and rubbed her hand on his head as if she were making a wish.

At breakfast, Pete couldn't stop looking at his dad's head. It looked like the egg in the little cup Dad had in front of him.

When Dad drove him to school, Pete could see Dad's
bald head sticking up over the back of the seat.
It looked like the sun poking up over the buildings.
Or a kickball stuck in the snow.

GOT BALD TIRES?

Chrome-dome Auto

After school, Dad took Pete for a haircut. The barber asked him, "Should I cut your hair like your father's?"

Pete put both hands on his head. "No way!" he said.

He didn't mean to make his dad feel bad, but Pete didn't want to be all bald on top.

"Just a trim will be fine," Dad told the barber.

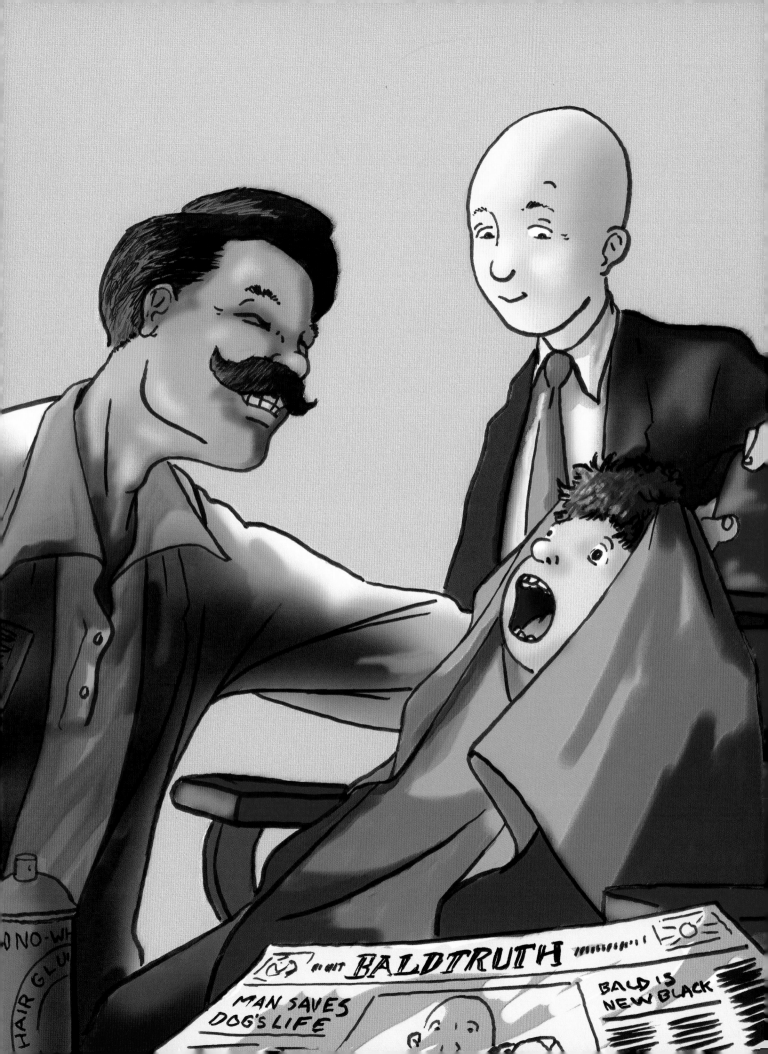

HAIR GLUE · NO-WH

BALDTRUTH

MAN SAVES
DOG'S LIFE

BALD IS
NEW BLACK

As they ran errands on the way home, Pete noticed the hair that other men had on their heads:

The man at the gas station had fake hair. When he picked up some coins from the floor, all his hair swung back and forth.

The man in the post office looked like someone had drawn lines on his head from one side to the other when he wasn't looking.

The man in the grocery store was bald on top but had fuzzy hair sticking out all around the edges. He looked like an ostrich.

Pete and his dad stopped at the park. Even though it was cold, Dad wore only the earmuffs Mom gave him for Christmas.

Pete felt sorry for him and put his hands on top of Dad's head to keep him warm.

"That feels good, kiddo," said Dad.

"With a son like you, who needs a hat?"

At home, Pete was very quiet.

"What's the matter, bub?" said his mom.

"Dad sure looks different without his hair," he said.

"Let me show you something," she said. She took out their picture album and showed Pete some old pictures of his dad from a long time ago—before Pete was born.

His father had lots of hair then. In one picture, his hair was as long as George Washington's on the dollar bill. Pete smiled. Dad sure looked funny.

"So, what do you think?" said his mom.

"I don't know," he said. The guy in those pictures looked even *less* like his dad.

When he put Pete to bed that night, Dad asked him, "Well, champ, how about it? Should I let my hair grow back, or do you like my new look?"

Pete looked at him closely.

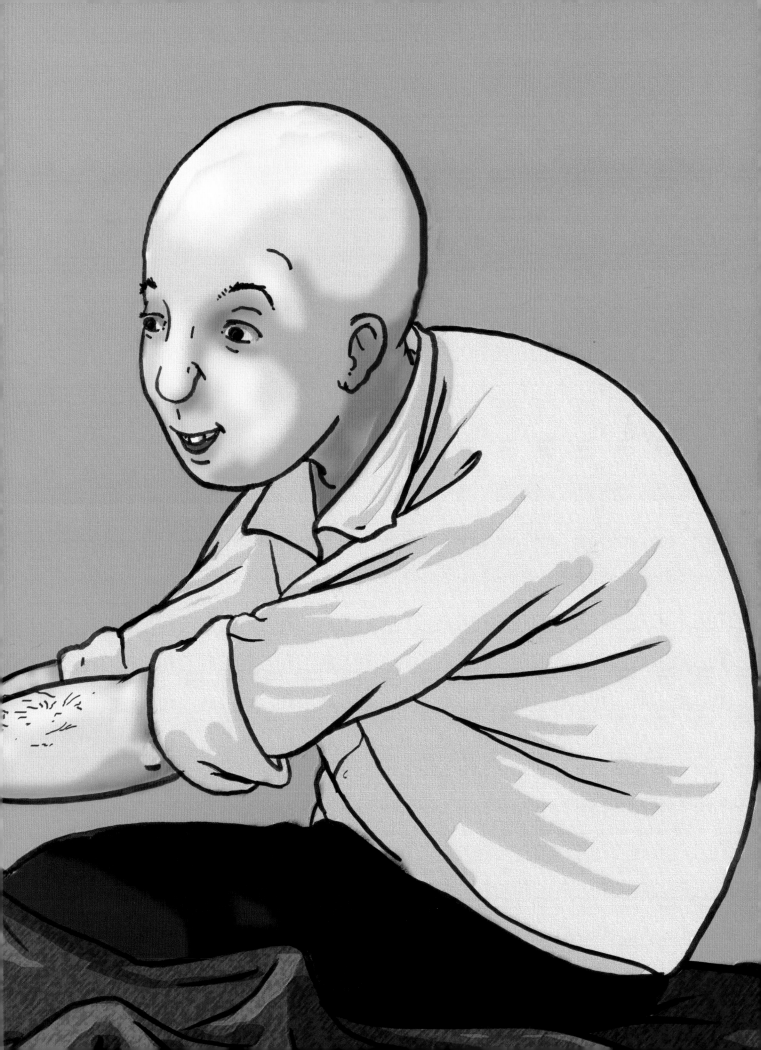

He thought about everything he'd seen that day with his dad: the men in the gas station and post office, the grocer, and the funny-looking man in the old pictures Mom had shown him.

SHAVE DOWN

He thought about how Dad looked in the morning with his scraggly bunch of weedy hairs.

"I guess it's okay," Pete said.

"With a son like you, who needs hair anyway?" said Pete's dad, and he kissed him good night.

"Wait a minute," said Pete, and he tilted his dad's head down and kissed him back.

Right on top of his shiny, bald head.

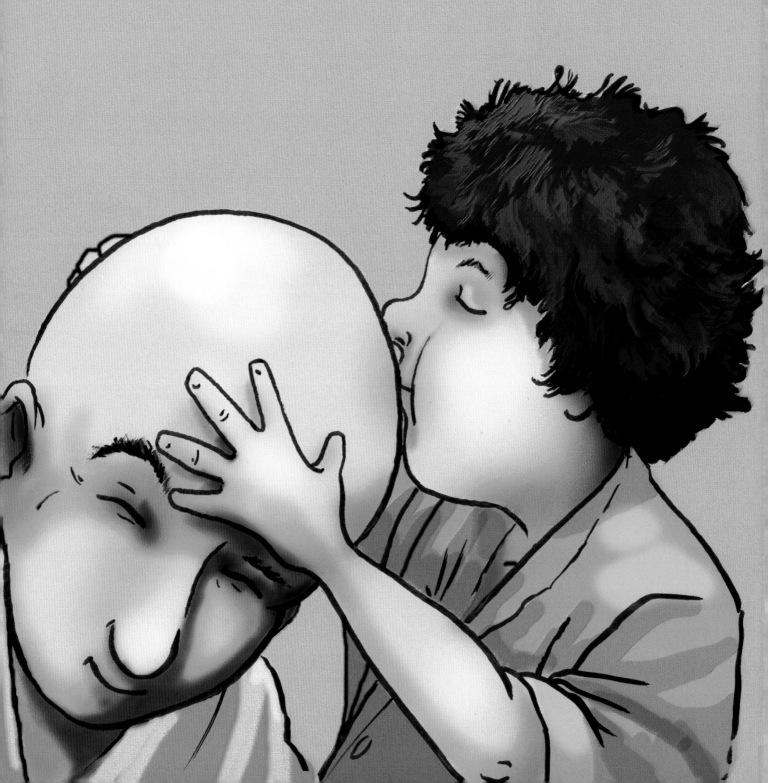

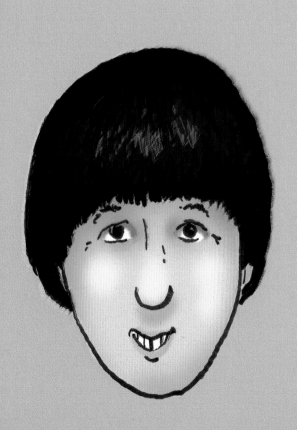